THE HOLIDAY HUSBAND

B. A. LOUDON

Beverley Loudon

THE HOLIDAY HUSBAND

ISBN: 978-1-9990560-9-4
The Holiday Husband

This book is a work of fiction and the product of watching too many Christmas movies. Any resemblance to people living or dead, or yet to come, is purely coincidental.

To my family –
Thank you for all your endless love and unbelievable support. Even Toby, who tried to erase this a few times by smashing the keys on my keyboard. Thanks, Buddy.
To Chelsey, Carl, Greg, and Oliver -
Thanks for being my betas on this, and projects to come. I'm just gonna send them to you. This is your life now.
To the real life Kristen, who would rather be in front of the camera than behind it -
If I manage to sell the rights to this, you can play yourself. I'll write it into my contract.

I

The small town of Everwinter Valley looked picturesque, like a Christmas card brought to life, and Carson Davis already hated it.

He hadn't even heard of it before this trip, and now that it lay before him, he knew why. It was small, pathetically small. It was surrounded by thick troves of snow covered evergreen trees, and seemingly nestled at the base of a mountain. The mountain was deceptive though; it was hours away, while the wooden sign greeted the vehicle as they entered the town.

All the buildings looked *old*. That was the best way Carson knew how to describe them. Well kept, he supposed, but *old*. It was as if time had left this poor desolate place behind, and no one had bothered to care. Wreaths and garlands and bows and other various holiday decor adorned every one, and though the daylight made it hard to spot, there was a plethora of lights strung between them all as well.

"C'mon, it's not so bad," the dark haired woman driving the van chided him with a smirk. "It's kind of cute, actually.

The kind of town you settle in when you give up all hope for life."

"Yeah, that seems accurate," he grumbled. "What a nightmare. This is a nightmare."

"Hey, don't blame me. We could be covering the Christmas celebrations in Hawaii. Warm and sunny and sandy..." She sighed. "Alas."

"Alas what, Kristen?" He looked at her accusingly as though he dared her to finish her thought.

She took that dare. "Alas, t'was not to be because *someone* - not *me* - pissed off the big guys."

"Yeah well, *someone* - not me - seems to have gotten us lost," he remarked as they passed a building that he could have sworn they'd been by at least once before. He hadn't noticed doing a loop, but it was tiny enough that it was possible.

"Feel free to help out. Do you see anything vaguely hotel looking?" She asked as she gestured over the steering wheel to the street before them.

"Use Google."

"Well now, *there* is a *gosh dang* good idea. I can't imagine why *I* didn't come up with such an *amazing, incredible* plan," Kristen replied sweetly, and her voice dripped with sarcasm.

"GPS isn't reading," he surmised. Excellent. The town was so dismal that even *Google* didn't want to be there.

"Indeed it is not so how about you make yourself useful," she said as she pulled the van over and parked on the street beside an old looking store, "and go in and ask?"

Carson looked out the window at the building in question. The sign, lettered in what he would describe as an 'old fashioned' style, read *Sweet Dave's Sweet Treats*. From the display featured in the oversized window, he surmised it to be a bakery. The structure itself looked like a combination of wood and stone, with a grand set of glass double doors. The entire thing looked as though it belonged on a movie set and not in real life.

He reluctantly opened the door and left the vehicle.

"How big is it gonna be this year, Dad?"

"Pretty big, Star!" Her father answered as he carefully pressed two icing covered edges of a gingerbread together. "I want to beat last year's."

"That's going to be hard, last year's one was really cool!" Stella grinned, watching him closely.

"It was cool, wasn't it?" He gingerly released his fingers and slowly lifted his hands away, making sure the two pieces held.

The bells above the front doors jingled, and the two turned to see an unfamiliar face walk through the door. He was a tall, blond haired man with an expensive looking long coat, and he also looked incredibly lost.

"Good morning," the baker greeted him as he stepped behind the shop's counter and wiped his hands on a towel. "Need directions?"

The newcomer looked embarrassed. "Is it that obvious?"

"Well you don't look like you're here to buy cupcakes," he joked. "Though if you are, I have the best ones around."

"I would hope so, going by the name of the shop," the other answered, pointing vaguely in the direction of the store sign. "And it's tempting, but you're right; I need directions."

"What brings you to town?" He asked, beckoning him over to the counter.

"I'm doing a story on..."

A loud squeal cut him off. "You're the reporter!" Stella exclaimed.

"Uh, yes," the man stammered before he regained a dignified composure. "Carson Davis," he extended his hand to the taller baker.

The other man looked exactly as Carson had imagined the average man in the town would look. He was tall, and built like the trees around. His hair and short beard were dark; all he was missing was a plaid shirt to complete the lumberjack look.

"Dave Sweet, like it says on the sign!" Dave shook his hand, before he gestured to the sandy blonde seven year old watching Carson with stars in her brown eyes. "That's Stella. She's been anxiously awaiting your arrival."

"I wanna be on tv!" She announced.

Carson chuckled nervously. "Is it big news that I'm here?"

"I mean, what isn't news in a small town?" Dave nodded and half shrugged. "Let's just say that some residents - like my Stella - are very eager to have you here."

"I see," he paused, as the mess of gingerbread pieces and full piping bags that were spread out on a large work table behind the glass displays caught his eye. There were a few buildings already finished, and the detail on them was incredible. They had what looked like glass windows, tiled roofs, and some were even painted to look like brick siding. "Besides the obvious, what's this?"

"This," Dave answered proudly, "is one of our traditions. We build a gingerbread model of the town centre. Every year it seems to get a little bigger, a little more detailed, and a little more time consuming."

Carson nodded, but looked a bit perplexed by the scale of it. "That's quite an undertaking."

"It is," Dave agreed, "but it's worth it! Now," he leaned forward on the wooden counter, which Carson noticed for the first time had a wood burned map of the town etched into it, "where can I point you?"

"The hotel, please."

"Thought so. It's a bit tricky, close to main street but not actually on main," the baker pointed to a spot on the map. "You want to go all the way down main, turn left here, go up two blocks, and then another left. You'll see it from there."

"Sounds good, thank you. Nice to meet you both," he waved awkwardly as he headed back out through the door.

The baker turned to his star-struck daughter and laughed. "What do you think, Star? You met your reporter, and he seems pretty nice, too."

"He's awesome!" She beamed as her tiny body nearly shook from the overwhelming excitement.. "Will we see him again?"

Her father shrugged. "I'm sure we'll see him around. C'mon, let's finish town hall today."

"That took long enough. Did you get lost *in* the building

too?" Kristen asked as her coworker got back into the van. "Is all hope lost?"

"They're building a giant gingerbread replica of the town," Carson replied, still amused at the idea.

"Oh sweet baby Jesus," Kristen started the van and shook her head. "All hope really *is* lost. Did I mention that we could be in *Hawaii* right now?"

"...and this one is your key, Mr. Davis," the hotel manager, a short, silver haired woman in her sixties with a name tag that read 'Elsie,' said as she passed the physical key to the waiting journalist.

"Charming," he said as he looked at the rather old fashioned key in his hands and forced a polite smile. Somehow, it suited everything else around him; dark stained wood flooring and paneling and... wood. So much woodwork.

"Yeah, the guests think so, that's why I haven't updated to electronic yet. I wanted to *years* ago," she confessed with a shrug. "There's a list of town amenities in your rooms, and the wifi password is written at the top of that, to save you the search."

Carson breathed a sigh of relief while his coworker

blurted out the thoughts he shared. "Oh thank God," she exclaimed, "*wifi!*"

Elsie smirked. "Yes, we do have *some* modern conveniences, contrary to popular belief. Through there," she pointed to a doorway on her left, "is the dining room. We offer service all day, and breakfast starts at seven thirty. I'd recommend coming earlier if you like quiet and fresh pastries."

"Are they from the bakery?" Carson asked. "We stopped there for directions. The owner bragged about cupcakes."

"Yes, in fact!" She smiled brightly. "Dave brings a fresh delivery every morning, and he wasn't lying about his cupcakes. They're as delightful as he is. Now," she pointed to her right, "that staircase there will take you up to the fourth floor. I put you up there to make sure you've got some privacy. Normally there's an elevator, but I'm afraid it's out of commission, unless you want to take a chance with your life."

It was tempting. "Thank you," he said with a smile, and grabbed his suitcase.

"Hold up," Kristen leaned on the front desk. "What's up with the baker? I see a lot of faces and you had a weird expression, and I have a need to know what it meant."

"Kristen," Carson hissed as he tried to elbow her, but she paid no heed.

"He's just a sweet man, matches his last name," Elsie replied with a fond smile. "He's had a rough hand dealt to him, and I'd like to see some good come his way."

"Like what?"

"Doesn't matter, not our business," Carson cut in, and grabbed her arm. He pulled her towards the stairs, and she waved to the owner and mouthed *I'll be back later.*

Carson sighed. It was going to be a long trip.

2

The morning air of six o'clock was still and quiet, the silence broken only by the occasional clacking of the keys on Carson's laptop. He sighed as he stared at the nearly empty document on screen and wished that he could somehow simply will a good story into existence.

'Make the town and it's festivities look appealing!' His boss's words echoed in his mind, taunting him. How the hell was he supposed to make this town look appealing when he hated everything about it? It was old. It was tacky. It was his failure.

It didn't help that whatever semblance that was left of his career was riding on this story.

The sleepy town of Everwinter Valley is filled to the brim with gaudy overdecoration and overzealous residents.

Maybe journalism wasn't the right career for him anyway. Maybe he should have just taken *the incident* as a sign and quit then. Sure, he would have then been stuck with a useless degree, student loans, and the remnants of his public humiliation, but at least he could have quietly faded into obscurity.

"You're up early!" The voice pulled Carson from his thoughts and startled him as he realized that he was no longer alone in the otherwise empty dining room. "I see you found the hotel."

"Yeah, I did, thanks to you," Carson replied as he looked up from his computer to see Dave dressed in a thick coat and carrying a large box in gloved hands. From the flush on his cheeks, he'd been out in the cold for a bit. "You're one to talk about being up early."

"I'm a baker, it comes with the territory," Dave said simply as he set the box down on a table and gave it a pat. "Gotta make my deliveries." He looked at the laptop in front of the other man. "You, uh, you working on the story?"

"Yeah," Carson exhaled deeply and slumped back in his seat. "Trying to, anyways."

"Have you been out to see the town yet?"

"No, not really." The most he had seen had been from the circles they had driven around main street while lost, not that there was really much to see anyways.

Dave folded his arms. "How could you write about it, then? Can't write about what you don't know."

"You make a good point," Carson admitted with a small laugh. "I have scheduled events that I'm supposed to cover in my segment. I figured I'd just build some framework around that first, though that doesn't seem to be working too well for me."

Dave grinned. "What's first up for your event coverage?"

The journalist flipped through his notes. "It looks like... snow sculptures tomorrow evening."

The baker frowned. "Not the light festival tonight?"

Carson couldn't hide a grimace. "Light festival? Aren't there enough lights hung up around here? Do you really need *more?*"

"You really didn't get out at all last night, did you?" Dave said teasingly, but Carson appreciated the playful, gentle tone.

"No," he admitted. "I unpacked, reflected on my life, and then came to the bar back there for further reflection. I guess I'm a bit of a scrooge about Christmas."

"I've been there," Dave replied honestly. "Anyways, if you had been out, you'd have seen a surprisingly dark town, apart from the streetlights; tonight's the night we officially turn all the Christmas lights *on,*" he explained. "It's short, but it's a big deal. Everyone gathers together in the town centre, mayor gives a speech, and then everyone waits for everything to come to life. And now, I have to ask, what's *your* reflection poison of choice?"

The question caught him off guard, but he answered just the same. "Depends on the kind of reflection. Usual? Beer. Last night? Anything stronger."

"Yeah, I get that, that's why I don't do a lot of reflection anymore," Dave sympathized. "Funny though, I had you pegged as a fancy champagne kind of guy, the kind that costs more than my mortgage."

Carson grimaced again. "I mean, I can *tolerate* it when I need to, but it's not something I'll go for willingly. Also, you overestimate how much I make." He cocked his head to the side and eyed the other man curiously. "Why the interest? Gonna ask me for a drink?"

"Maybe, or maybe I'm just nosey," Dave replied with a shrug. "Stella's in love with the idea of being on TV, I'd love to pick your brain a bit about that." Right, for *Stella*; Dave wasn't sure he believed that himself, the other man certainly wouldn't. "Speaking of, why don't you come with her and I tonight? We can be your tour guides if you want to see any more of the town afterwards, and you'd make her night."

The offer was appealing, though he wasn't sure how his colleague would react to it. Then again, she was the one who had chosen to sleep in and wasn't with him to make the decision. How could she blame him for being proactive and securing them a lead for their assignment? Really, he was just being responsible.

"Apparently I need some tour guides," Carson accepted gratefully. "Thank you. My colleague will be with me, I'm not in town alone," he explained as he realized for the first time that he hadn't said as much previously. "If that's all right?"

"The more the merrier! Stella will be thrilled," Dave beamed, suddenly feeling a bit merrier himself. "We'll meet you in the town square around 5, if you can find it."

He chuckled. "Yeah, I think I can find that. Just a bit up from your bakery?"

"That's right," he confirmed as he headed back towards the door. "See you later!" He waved over his shoulder as he walked out through the lobby and left the building.

Carson returned the wave, and then looked back to his computer screen.

"Was that Dave I heard?" Elsie asked as she looked out from behind the kitchen door.

"Yeah, he left a package on that table," Carson answered her, pointing to the cardboard box ahead of him. "Want me to bring it to you?"

"No, that's alright, but thank you!" The older woman made her way over to the delivery and picked it up with ease.

She glanced quickly at the journalist to see him smiling softly to himself. Careful not to let him see her face, she smirked knowingly to herself as she took the package back to the kitchen.

Carson thought for a moment, and then tapped to erase the line in the document.

3

"You should have brought gloves," Kristen chided the shivering man next to her. "I mean, who comes to a town named *Everwinter Valley*, and doesn't bring gloves?"

"I didn't think of them," Carson admitted bitterly before he blew into his folded hands to warm them. "I was packing in a hurry. And angry."

"Rage packing," she surmised, her breath visible in the frosty evening air. Unlike her friend, she hadn't forgotten any winter gear. Her stylish black coat was leather, as were the gloves on her hands. Carson suspected that if she'd been able to find a leather beanie, she would have been wearing that instead of the blue knit one on her head. "Been there. Why don't you ask your new friend if he's got any extra gloves?"

"New friend?"

"Y'know, the eligible bachelo-- I mean, baker."

Carson raised an eyebrow. "What exactly are you implying?" Before she could answer, he waved her away with his hand. "Actually you know what? I don't care. Why don't you focus on doing your job and getting some B roll shots?"

Kristen laughed but turned her camera to the darkened town. "Mmm yeah, darkness. Riveting television."

"Carson!" The excited voice of a seven year old broke through the crowd moments before she did.

"I see you've got at least one fan left," Kristen noted as a pink coated Stella barreled towards them, the girl's father not far behind.

"Sorry to keep you waiting," Dave panted as he finally caught up with his energetic daughter. "We lost track of time with the town."

"I bet, it looks like it would be time consuming," Carson said in agreement.

"It's looking really cool, Carson! We did lots today! You should come see it!" She told him excitedly as she tugged on his coat sleeve. The girl suddenly noticed the other person standing with them. "Who are you?"

"Only the lifeblood of this entire operation," she answered.

"This is Kristen, my camera man," Carson introduced them while giving his longtime friend a pointed look.

Stella frowned and looked Kristen over. "But she's a girl."

"Ah, observant little thing!" Kristen grinned.

"Camera *woman*," Carson corrected himself as Dave and Kristen shook hands in introduction. "When do things get going around here?" He asked as he checked the time on his phone. He worried about sounding impatient, but his body protested being in the cold.

"Should be soon," Dave scanned out over the crowd, and pointed to the far end. "That's the mayor out over there, you'll probably want to meet with her soon."

Carson squinted to see where he was pointing. He could vaguely make out the dark skinned woman from where he was standing. She seemed to be gesturing as she spoke, but none of them could hear what she was saying. "Yeah, we have a meeting set up with her for tomorrow, this was supposed to be our settling in day."

"Heh, sorry to wreck that for you," the baker apologized. "I do think you'll enjoy this."

The journalist was about to reassure him when the crowd near the front began to chant, and the rest caught on. "15! 14! 13!"

"You'll want to get this!" Dave told Kristen excitedly. He turned back to Carson, and noticed the man's red hands for the first time. "Why don't you have gloves? Your hands must be numb!"

Carson felt his face flush and his heart race. "I-I..."

Before he could form a coherent sentence, the other man had pulled off his own gloves and taken Carson's hands between his own to warm them. His hands were larger than the journalist's, and softer than Carson had expected. The unprepared man felt a pleasant but unexpected warmth spread through his entire body, not simply his hands.

He looked up into the baker's gentle brown eyes.

"3!"

"2!"

"1!"

All around them, the town sparked to life.

Soft whites and blues seemed to dance in the air, and multi-colour flashes sparkled around the two men. He hadn't noticed all the lights strung above them between the buildings on the street when they had arrived, but they were impossible to miss now. The street had become almost a tunnel of lights, encasing them in dazzling wonder.

Carson couldn't help but look around in amazement. For all his cynicism, it really was a beautiful sight.

For the briefest of moments, everyone else gathered faded away and Carson and Dave stood together, breathless.

It crashed to an end as Stella shouted, "Look at all the lights, Dad!"

"Uh, yeah, they're... they're pretty neat," Dave answered flusteredly as the two men pulled apart. He cleared his throat. "Here, uh, take my gloves. My pockets will do just fine for now."

"Thank you," Carson's face burned more than his hands, but he accepted the offer. He made a point not to look Kristen's way.

"Do *you* like the lights, Carson?" Stella asked.

"Yes, I do," He admitted truthfully as he took another look around.

"We're going to keep decorating cookies after!" The little girl told him proudly. "You should come too!" Before the journalist could answer, Stella had tugged on her Dad's arm. "Can Carson come decorate cookies too?"

"Sure, if he wants to. You're welcome to come too," Dave added to Kristen.

"Thanks, but no thanks," she replied as she tucked her camera back into the bag at her side. "I don't think that's really my thing, and I need to get some extra footage of the town. Different angles."

"Carson?" Stella asked expectantly.

"I..." He started to answer, and Kristen subtly nudged him in the ribs. "Yes, alright, why not?"

"Hey, not bad!" Dave said approvingly as Carson carefully squeezed the icing bag in his hands.

The other man scoffed but grinned. "Not great either," he replied as he focused intently on the lines he piped on to the cookie surface before him. "You make this look easy. Both of you."

"Stella's been helping me decorate since before she could walk, cut yourself a little slack. Right, Star?"

His daughter nodded. "I've done lots of cookies!" Stella beamed proudly. "Probably a million!"

"I don't know about a million," her dad laughed, "but lots for sure."

"Do you always stick out your tongue when you decorate

cookies?" Stella asked and giggled at the man trying his best to not make a complete mess.

Carson stopped and looked up at the girl. "Was I sticking out my tongue?" He asked in bewilderment.

"Yes!" Stella answered gleefully. "It's funny!"

He laughed. "You'd think for someone who's on camera all the time, I'd be more aware of what my mouth was doing."

Stella propped her chin on her palms and looked at Carson inquisitively from across the work table. "What's it like being on TV?"

Carson took a moment to consider his words carefully and swallowed heavily. "It's... okay," he said finally. "It's a job, not always a fun one."

"Why?" She looked crestfallen, something he'd been trying to avoid. He kicked himself internally and set into damage control.

"Oh, I mean, sometimes it's lots of fun. Like right now, for example! This is sort of part of my job because I'm in town for work, and I get to learn how to decorate gingerbread cookies." This seemed to brighten her spirits and the seven year old perked up in her seat. "Some days, I even get to spend my time eating things like this!" He glanced towards the girl who was happily hanging on to his every word.

So was her father, who sensed the missing word. "But...?"

Carson sighed. "But, sometimes - a lot of the time, actually - there's a lot of pressure. And sometimes, you mess up. The problem with messing up on TV is that it's not a private mistake; everyone sees it."

Stella frowned and was quiet as she mulled the new information over. "That sucks!" She finally announced, and both men laughed.

"Yeah, it does," the journalist agreed. "It really does."

Carson sat at the empty table and allowed his thoughts to wander. Above him, he could hear the floorboards creak as Dave put Stella to bed. She had tried valiantly to protest bedtime, but her father had won in the end. He thought it was neat that they lived in an apartment above the bakery; Carson couldn't imagine living so close to his workplace.

Then again, his workplace was anywhere it needed or happened to be.

The bakery around him was quiet, and the warm lights dimmed apart from the one above him. It was so far away from what he was used to, but it was sort of nice, he supposed. The front doors were locked and all the displays were empty, but the windows only had blinds, and they weren't even fully closed. No security system, no heavy barring or steel shutters... it didn't seem to be needed.

"I'm sorry Stella is so nosey," Dave apologized as he set a large mug of hot chocolate down in front of Carson and pulled him back to reality. "She's just enamored with the idea of being on television."

"I don't mind," Carson replied truthfully. "I hope I didn't destroy her dream too badly, but I wanted to be honest with her."

"I appreciate that, I know it's not as glamorous as she thinks, but she's seven. She doesn't understand all that yet," Dave said, and Carson raised his eyebrows in agreement as he took a careful sip. "I feel like there's a story behind the warning about messing up?" The other man nodded. "So?"

"*So*, I see where Stella gets the nosiness from," Carson replied with a smile before sighing. "Yeah, it uh, it's why I'm here, actually. In Everwinter Valley. I'm on thin ice with the network, and they thought a feel good Christmas piece would help my public image out."

"Do you think it will?"

He shrugged. "I have no idea, but I'm hoping it improves *their* image of me. I want to get back to my usual assignments.

I don't normally do the Christmas presentations. This was also intended as somewhat of a punishment for me."

Dave leaned back in his chair. "What do you usually cover?"

"Not feel-good stories, that's for sure," Carson laughed a little to himself. "Crime mostly. Sometimes politics. Sometimes both of those at once, if I'm lucky. I usually cover the high profile cases, murder and such."

"Interesting. Grim, but interesting," Dave nodded to himself. "Alright," he said after a drink, "your turn."

"My turn?"

"To be nosey. You are a journalist after all, it should be your thing."

"Hmm," Carson thought for a moment. He didn't know much about the baker, or about the town itself. He had a plethora of options, but his mind drew a blank. "Why do you call Stella, 'Star?' Is it the TV thing?" Carson asked finally.

"No, it goes back way farther," Dave smiled sadly at a distant memory. "When she was a baby, she had this obnoxious bright yellow snowsuit. My late husband always said that it made her..."

"Look like a star," Carson finished, and the baker nodded.

"I'm sorry," he said after a moment of silence. "How did he pass?" He asked, and immediately regretted it. "I'm sorry, that's too personal and not my busi..."

"Cancer," Dave answered. "It was quick, which was both a blessing, and the worst imaginable thing. Alan didn't suffer long, but we didn't have long to really say goodbye." Dave gave a long sigh. "It's been six years, but sometimes it still feels like yesterday. Other times it feels like it was another lifetime."

Although he had been fortunate enough to not know the pain the other man had experienced, Carson nodded. He placed a consoling hand on Dave's arm, and got a soft smile in return.

They sat like that a while, in a comfortable silence.

4

"So," Carson raised his eyes from his laptop screen to see his friend smirking at him over her coffee cup, "you got back late last night."

"It wasn't that late, maybe 11," Carson replied defensively. "We decorated cookies and lost track of time."

Her prying gaze stayed on him. "...Annnnnnnnd?"

"And drank hot chocolate," he informed her. "Whatever juice you're looking for isn't here. There was nothing scandalous." Kristen made a humming noise that he knew meant that she didn't believe him. "Look, I brought my cookie back with me, I can show you it!"

She still didn't look convinced, so he decided to change the subject before the interrogation continued. "What'd you get for footage last night?"

"Usable footage, as always," she replied. "A few crowd shots, though I tried to keep the focus on the lights. Something about Christmas lights makes people feel all warm and fuzzy, and I know that's what the bosses want for this."

"Perfect," the keys on the laptop clacked away as he made some notes. "Did you get the moment that the lights turned on? Like a crowd reaction?"

"Sure did. I'm a professional."

"Alright," Carson sat back in his chair, "so this is what I'm thinking. We use the lights turning on as the opening shot for this whole piece, and it leads into the start of the monologue. We can do a segment of me walking around during the sculpture competition."

His colleague nodded as she pictured it. "Do you have the monologue written?"

"Not exactly. I have a rough idea. We can record what I do have, and we can also record just me walking through and dub over it if needed." Kristen raised her eyebrows. "Look we're not creating anything to win awards, just something to entertain, and keep our jobs." And, hopefully, something to restore his credibility in the eyes of the network executives.

"*And keep our jobs,*" she repeated his words back to him for emphasis, and took a sip of her coffee. "Or, your job anyways. I think I'm still fairly safe."

"Gee, thanks. Your concern is, as always, heartwarming."

Behind them, the door to the hotel opened and a familiar sight walked in with a large box.

Kristen looked over her shoulder to see who had come in; she'd had an idea from the way Carson's eyes had lit up. Once confirmed, she looked back to Carson with a smirk and dumped the remainder of her coffee into his empty cup. "Oh my heavens, would you look at that," she said dramatically, "I'm all out of coffee. I guess I just have to venture out for some more, gosh darn."

"Smooth," Carson rolled his eyes. "You know, you can just call Elsie for a refill... or not," he finished as the dark haired woman was already gone, having ducked into the kitchen of the hotel. "You're later than yesterday," he greeted Dave as the baker ambled his way into the dining room.

"Yeah, well, I had a late night," Dave replied with a good natured smile. "How's the story going?"

"It's..." Carson looked at his half-filled screen. "It's a work in progress."

"Isn't everything?"

"Yeah, I suppose," the journalist agreed with a grin. "It's coming along. A work in progress, but at least there is some progress."

"I told you it would help to see the town!" Dave teased, and Carson nodded.

"You were correct, thank you for that," Carson replied as he raised his newly filled mug in a toast. "Actually, last night was really nice," he added sincerely.

Dave went to speak, but hesitated a moment. "I'm sorry about part of it, though," he finally blurted out.

Carson frowned. "What for?"

"Oh, uh, y'know, all the dead husband stuff. It was a bit heavy. I don't usually talk about him, but it just kind of..."

"I don't mind," Carson assured him quickly. "I really don't. I was the one who asked anyways." He tilted his head and studied the baker's face; his expression was a mixture of what seemed to be embarrassment and grief. "For what it's worth, it's obvious that you loved him very much."

"I did," Dave replied, "and I do. I... I always will. It's complicated."

Carson couldn't help the smile that spread across his face. "Isn't everything?"

Dave chuckled. "Heh, yeah, you got me there." He cleared his throat. "Right, uh, I better finish all my rounds. As you pointed out, I'm already late today. I'll see you later, at ice skating and snow sculpting? You did pack skates, right?"

"I don't actually own any," Carson admitted. "I live in LA, not really much use for them."

"But you have been skating before, right?"

"Not in a while, wasn't really planning on it tonight."

Dave shook his head sadly and placed his hand on his chest. "You're going to break poor Stella's heart."

The kitchen doors burst open. "Don't you worry, we'll get him all set up," Kristen announced as she came back to the table. "Can't have that sweet kiddo disappointed now, can we?"

"Right," Carson forced a smile.

"Alright then!" Dave beamed. "I'll see you at the rink tonight!"

As Dave waved to them and left, the journalist's smile dropped and he glared at Kristen. "Really? How long were you listening?"

"Oh, only from where he said he had to get going," Kristen replied confidently, but unconvincingly. "Lighten up, you're gonna have a great time."

He groaned. "You're a pain sometimes, you know that?"

"A *professional* pain," she corrected with a grin.

"I can't believe that you volunteered me for this," Carson grumbled as the pair walked along main street to make their way back to the hotel.

"Well, it's like that old saying. When in Everwinter Valley, do as the people who live here do. Besides," she lifted her own shopping bag gleefully, "You needed gloves and a hat, and I wanted to get my own skates anyways. It's been ages and it'll be legitimately fun. Plus I can get some cool shots."

"I didn't know you skated," her friend stated. "Learn something new every day."

"I'm Canadian, dude, of course I skate."

The statement caught him off guard. "Wait, really?"

Kristen huffed. "How long have we worked together now? Five, maybe six years, and you didn't know?"

He shrugged. "I don't know what to tell you. I guess we just don't really talk about our personal lives all that much, despite the fact that you're one of my best friends. You and Ana."

She nudged him softly in the arm. "Awe, thanks you big softy. It's mutual, at least on my end. Can't speak for our famous friend though. But, I guess we just haven't really had personal lives, not until now, anyways."

Carson groaned. "Oh, not this again."

Kristen beamed. "Not what again?"

"I didn't come here to a stupid small town to find love, I came here for work, is that what you want to hear?" Carson asked.

"I think you'll find that that is the exact opposite of what I want to hear," she replied. "You need to work on your multi-tasking. There's no reason you can't work *and* find love. Plus, you don't really think this is a stupid little town. *I* still think that, but *you* don't."

"I admit, it certainly has more charm than I initially thought," he conceded. "It's peaceful, and slow moving, and yeah, it's been a nice change. No one here, apart from maybe Stella, knows who I am. Better yet, no one seems to *care*. Even the mayor, look how she was this morning; you can tell she looked me up but she has no opinions about the incident. It's like they're all seeing me for the first time, like the last six months didn't really happen."

Kristen could see how that would be appealing for him, but it jogged her memory. "Did you check your email recently?"

"No since this morning, no," Carson replied, and stopped in his tracks. "Why?"

"How do you feel about spending Christmas Eve here?"

"Oh no," he didn't like where this was going. "What now?"

"They want to do a live broadcast on Christmas eve, check in with everyone from wherever they all are," she told him. "They think it'll be a good ratings boost, kind of like a New Year's Eve broadcast... but a week early."

Carson cursed under his breath. "Great," he finally said as he started walking again. "I love getting more added to my plate. Love it."

"Yeah, I thought you would," she gave him a pat on the back. "I thought you would."

5

"How tight are these supposed to be, again?" Carson asked, pulling on the laces of his new skates. At the shop, the salesperson had laced them for him, and he had been surprised at how tight they felt. On the cold bench outside, he had a hard time replicating that feeling.

"Ideally, you should have little to no feeling in your feet," his friend replied jokingly.

"Right," he said, giving them another tug. "Do you need to be filming right now?"

"Uh yeah, of course I do," she answered, looking at the view screen. "This assignment is supposed to help improve your image, right? People are going to want to see you involved in everything, participating in all the..." she waved her free hand about as she searched for the right words. "...Christmas shenanigans. Now come on, give the camera a nice big smile!"

Carson turned and smiled as he tied off his skate, but dropped it the moment he turned his head away. He raised his eyes to the rink and swallowed, despite his mouth feeling unusually dry. It seemed as if the entire town was out skating that night on the large community ice; seniors, teenagers, even toddlers, all whizzed around with more skill than Carson knew he possessed.

He tried to get to his feet and immediately regretted it.

"I may need some help," he admitted sheepishly.

The dark haired woman smirked and shook her head, but turned off her camera and stuck it in the grey bag that was slung over her shoulder. She held out her hand, and pulled her friend slowly to his feet. Carson wobbled rather ungracefully and clung tightly to her arm.

"Easy bud, baby steps," she coached him as they carefully made their way to the rink's opening. "You gonna be okay on the ice?"

"Oh yeah... I hope so, anyways," Carson replied as his sense of balance quickly betrayed him. "Just don't film me if I'm not."

"Oh I still will, but don't worry; I'll just keep that footage for my personal collection," she teased, but the journalist wasn't convinced that it was entirely a joke.

Once they got to the entrance, he traded Kristen's arm for

the sideboard and inched his way onto the ice. His legs continued to shake like a newborn fawn beneath him.

Kristen glided onto the ice with ease. "I'm going to go grab some crowd shots, and hopefully some of you once you find your hockey legs. If you get into any trouble, I'm sure there's a hospital or something nearby. Maybe."

"Ha, ha," Carson replied sarcastically as the woman skated off.

He held onto the wall of the rink for stability as he tried desperately to find his balance. One foot slowly moved forward, then the other.

Right foot.

Left foot.

Right.

Left.

Right.

Left.

Slow and steady.

"Doing great, buddy!" Kristen called as she zoomed past

him. He scoffed; he wasn't doing great, and they both knew it, but at least her encouragement seemed somewhat sincere.

Finally, he felt brave enough to let go of the siding and try to skate on his own. Carson straightened up his posture and held his head high, only to immediately hunch forward again when he felt himself losing control. At least in a town like this, there probably weren't any paparazzi to capture his utter failure on skates and make him a national laughing stock once more.

There was just Kristen, and her camera.

He wasn't sure which was worse.

"You doing okay?" He heard Dave's voice call. Carson looked up to see the other man skating to a stop with ease.

"If I said yes, you wouldn't believe me," Carson replied, trying to stand up straight once again so the baker wouldn't think less of him, "but I haven't fallen yet, so that's something."

"That's great! Small victories!" Dave laughed warmly.

It appeared that Carson had spoken too soon. Without warning, he felt himself begin to topple backwards and his arms flailed involuntarily as he seemed to fall in slow motion. Luckily for him, Dave was quick to action and caught the falling journalist in his arms.

"Thank you," Carson wheezed gratefully, his cheeks turning a deep crimson. His heart raced wildly, and he wasn't sure if it was from the adrenaline of nearly falling, or the adrenaline from being caught by the handsome bearded baker.

"No worries!" Dave helped the other man back to his feet, and Carson couldn't help but notice the slight flush in Dave's face as well.

"I think I'm done," Carson admitted defeat. "White flag. Surrender. Ice wins."

"Oh, c'mon now."

He shook his head. "I don't want to end up on Kristen's private tapes."

Dave blinked. "Uh, okay, I'm not sure what that means but I do know that I can't let you miss out on the magic that is ice skating."

The blond shook his head. "I think I've had my fill of this magic."

"You haven't experienced it a bit yet! C'mon, I'll help you," Dave offered, holding out his hand.

Carson reluctantly agreed, and grabbed the offered hand. They went slow at first, and Carson slowly found the rhythm

of the ice below him. Push off with one foot and glide forward. Repeat with other foot.

Push.

Glide.

Push.

Glide.

Dave looked as proud as Carson was starting to feel.
"That's it!" The baker looked out over the rink at the thinning
crowd. "I want to try something - do you trust me?"

"Depends, what for?" The other asked skeptically.

"You'll find out."

"Okay, sure… I trust you," Carson said, and hoped that he
wouldn't regret his words.

Dave let go of his hand, and skated so that he was behind
the other man. The baker's hands gripped Carson's waist, and
he began to skate forwards, gradually increasing his speed.
Soon the pair were zipping around the rink with Dave fully
in control.

Carson couldn't help laughing loudly as he spread his arms
out as though he were flying, which was a bit how he felt. The

wind rushed past him as they danced on the ice. It was fast, and graceful, and absolutely exhilarating.

He finally understood what Dave meant by the magic.

"Thank you for that," Carson said as the two walked - now in regular boots - towards the snow sculpture area. He held a paper cup full of hot chocolate in one hand, and carried the bag with his skates in the other.

"You needed to experience that to truly get the full Everwinter Valley Christmas experience," Dave replied simply. "It's a lot of fun on Christmas Eve as well, if you're still around."

"I will be," Carson confirmed. "I'm actually supposed to be doing a live broadcast from here on Christmas Eve. I'm not sure what on yet. Maybe skating. Who knows, maybe one day I'll even be able to skate on my own?"

"Think you'll pick it up in LA? You have your own pair now," Dave said, gesturing to the tote bag before he took a sip of his own drink.

Carson shrugged. "Maybe? Or maybe I'll just come back to visit for lessons. There's a great teacher living here, and this town has a sort of charm that grows on you after a while." And no prying eyes - he liked that as well.

Dave chucked to himself. "Hey, uh, speaking of LA, what was your big mistake?"

"Oh, I see Mr. Nosey is out again tonight," Carson said teasingly. "Honestly, just google me. It'll be your first result, I guarantee it." He couldn't help the bitterness that slipped into his voice. "One mistake and no one remembers any of the other work you've done."

"I'd much rather hear it from you."

"I'd much rather not talk about it," he replied glumly. "Sorry."

"Nah, it's alright. I just thought I'd try," Dave waved dismissively. "You're right about Stella getting her nosiness from me. It really isn't my business."

"Speaking of, where is she?"

"She entered the kid's sculpture contest."

Carson raised an eyebrow. "Oh really? But I thought I'd break her heart if I didn't come ice skating."

Dave grinned sheepishly. "Oh, did I say Stella? I meant it would have broken *my* heart."

"Oh, well, couldn't have that either," Carson replied.

"In fact, uh... Stella hates skating," her father admitted, and the two laughed at the absurdity of it.

"Oh, it's snowing," Carson said as he looked at the gentle white flakes in the air. They swirled and danced daintily on a breeze that he hadn't yet noticed until that moment.

Dave quietly watched the other man, and relished the childlike wonder. "I bet you don't see snow a lot, do you?"

"No, not like this, anyways," he replied. There was a sort of serenity about it that he found himself drawn to. For just a brief period of time, he had no worries or thoughts of work plaguing his mind; It was just him and Dave, and a blissful stillness that encapsulated everything.

Dave linked his arm with Carson's, and they enjoyed the moment together.

"I still can't believe they want a live broadcast," Carson groaned as he rubbed his temples.

Kristen swirled the milk in her coffee around with a spoon. "Are you really *that* surprised? I'm mostly just surprised they gave us so much advance notice.

He couldn't really argue with that; this new development wasn't out of character for the network in the slightest. "I'm mostly just annoyed. I have no idea where to do it, what to feature.... Would carolers be too cliche?" He asked miserably.

Kristen nodded, her mouth full of pastry. "Yes, absolutely, one hundred percent," she said as she dusted the crumbs from her hands. "Though, it will work as a last resort. Round up some kids for the *awwww* factor and we're practically guaranteed a viral hit."

"We'd have to get Stella if we went that route, she'd be furious otherwise," he mused as he lifted his coffee mug to his lips.

Kristen suddenly slammed her hands down on the table-top. "That's it!" She exclaimed excitedly.

Carson clutched his mug tightly and stared wide eyed at her. "What is?"

She seemed smugly pleased with whatever idea had entered her brain. "Listen, not only will this be great, it'll also give you an excuse to spend more time with your baker."

Carson rolled his eyes, but listened intently as she explained.

The bells above the bakery door jingled brightly as Carson walked into the shop.

"Hi Carson!" Stella called happily to the journalist from the back of the bakery.

"Hold on, Star," Dave cautioned from his place atop a large metal ladder. She quickly grabbed the bottom to steady it. "Need directions somewhere?" He asked the journalist teasingly.

"Actually, I come with a proposal of sorts," Carson replied, watching the baker reach into a large box that was precariously perched on the very top of the ladder. "Is this a bad time?"

"Not if the ring's big enough!" He joked back.

"Not that kind of proposal," Carson grinned. "Sorry to burst your bubble."

"Well, I expect a certain blue box when it is."

"You *really* overestimate my salary," he replied as he watched Dave straighten back up and eye the low wooden beam in front of him. "What are you guys doing?"

"Hanging mistletoe to make people kiss!" Stella told him with delight.

"Other decorations too!" Dave protested. "But I do enjoy catching couples off guard. Call me a soft old romantic," he said, taping the sprig in his hand to what he deemed to be the perfect spot on the beam. "The problem is that I get a lot of repeat customers, so I have to move it around a lot. I don't want people to know where it is."

"That makes sense," Carson nodded as the baker descended back down the ladder.

"I like to think so. So what's this proposal?"

Carson beamed. "I think you're going to like this. I hope you are anyways." Dave leaned against the countertop and listened with curiosity. "I told you last night that I have to do that live broadcast on Christmas Eve?" The baker nodded. "I want to feature your gingerbread town!"

"My gingerbread town?" He repeated, and the journalist nodded.

"It's a beautiful work of art, Dave," he told the other man sincerely. "It deserves to be spotlighted, and I'd like you and Stella to do a live grand reveal!"

Stella gasped loudly and covered her face with her hands in surprise. "I get to be on TV?!"

"Only if your Dad says it's okay, but I'd like you to be."

The girl clasped her hands together and looked pleadingly at her father. "Please, Dad? Oh please please please please!"

Carson crouched down beside her and copied her pose. "Oh please please please!"

"Oh no, no that's not fair, you can't play the Stella card against me," he protested.

Carson shrugged. "Call us even, then."

"What card?" Stella asked, her face scrunched in confusion. "I don't have a card."

"Nevermind, Star, it's a figure of speech."

Carson studied the baker's expression, trying to read it as he waited eagerly for a response. "So... what do you say?"

"I'd be honoured," Dave replied. "But are you sure? My little creation?"

"Are you kidding? It's amazing, and I wouldn't exactly call it little," Carson added, gesturing to the long table that it currently resided on. He took Dave's hand and held it between both of his own. "You're really talented, and I want to showcase that. You deserve it."

The two shared an intimate gaze, simultaneously standing too close yet too far away from one another.

"Thank you," Dave said softly, and cleared his throat as they awkwardly pulled apart. "Hey, uh, you sticking around for a while? You're welcome to help us finish with the decorations."

"I'd love to," Carson answered honestly, "but I'm afraid I have plans. Kristen and I are off on a snowshoe adventure to get some good footage. The sports shop told us about some good trails around here, so we figured why not?"

The baker laughed. "Seems like you two have been enjoying yourselves."

"I can't speak for Kristen, but I have been." It was a weird thing to admit out loud, but it was true; he really *had* been enjoying his time there, despite everything.

"You guys are just renting shoes, I take it."

"Yeah, Kristen's picking them up right now," Carson explained. "I'm not sure I'm going to have much use for skates in LA, I definitely wouldn't have any use for snowshoes!"

7

"I'll bet this is another first?" Dave asked the other man with the shared blanket bundled over his lap. The rhythm of the gait of the two horses pulling the sleigh caused the men to sway back and forth, and occasionally bounce over bumps.

"A bit of one, yeah," Carson replied honestly. "I've been horseback riding before, believe it or not. Never a sleigh ride though! I never thought I'd be living *Jingle Bells* the day before Christmas Eve."

"I'm surprised that Kristen isn't up there with Marshall," Dave gestured to the very front of the long sleigh to where an older man sat up high, reins in hand. "Don't you need footage of this for your story?"

"We actually submitted everything to the network yesterday," Carson said, relief evident on his face. "This... this is for me. And I enjoy your company, so that's a bonus," he grinned. "It's nice to do something because *I want* to, you know?"

The other man was quiet a moment, and then chuckled

softly as he scratched his beard under his chin. "Y'know, you remind me of Alan sometimes." He coughed and flusteredly tried to backtrack. "Wait, sorry, I just made it weird. I do think you would have liked him though."

"I'm sure I would have," he smiled back. "What reminds you of him?" He asked curiously. "My TV good looks? My wit and charm? My ability to torpedo my entire career in under three minutes?"

"You don't look anything like him," Dave clarified with a laugh. "No, uh, it's the way you encourage me to do things for myself. It's just been Stella and I for so long, the truth is that I haven't done anything for *me* for a long time."

Carson wasn't entirely surprised by that. He looked out to the softly lit path they were travelling down. "What about the bakery?" He asked as he turned back to the man beside him.

The baker looked uncomfortable, but not at the question. "I'm a trained pastry chef," he finally said, "I used to work for Elsie in-house. Alan used to say that I needed my own bakery, that it was the next step in my career. I wasn't sure I wanted that kind of responsibility, y'know? My own business. That was especially true after Stella was born; I didn't want to be away from her more than I had to."

"What changed?"

"Alan got sick, as you know, and he..." Dave's voice broke.

"With it being so quick, we were lucky, in a sense. He didn't end up with a lot of medical bills, and he'd already inherited a sizable estate from his parents. The only family he had left - besides me and Stella - was his sister. She was willed a part of his estate, but she wanted it put into a trust for Stella, so that's what happened with that." He cleared his throat. "Sorry, I uh, I'm rambling."

"It's okay," Carson assured him gently. "So is that when you opened the bakery?"

He nodded. "Alan left me a letter with his will, and told me to start the bakery with the money, to follow my dream." Dave sighed. "More of his dream, really."

"So you did it to honour him?" Carson asked.

"Yeah, I almost felt like I had to." Dave cleared his throat once more. "I'm sorry, that sounds awful. I... He just wanted me to be happy, as was his way."

"You don't have to explain how you feel. Feelings are rarely rational," Carson cut in. "But are you? Happy, that is?"

Dave pursed his lips. "I want to be," he admitted, "and sometimes, I am! But, it's a process."

"I get that."

The two horses pulling the sleigh turned, and they left the

forested path and turned onto a paved road. The town came into view, lit up beautifully against the dark of the night.

"Wow," Carson breathed.

"Isn't she a sight?" Dave asked proudly as he took in the serene awe on the other man's face. "I have to say, it's been great watching you experiencing everything here. It's almost like you're experiencing *Christmas* for the first time."

Carson chuckled. "That's kind of what it feels like."

The pair listened to the sound of hooves on the asphalt, and watched as the town grew nearer.

"Thank you," Dave said after a moment.

"For what?"

"I feel like I've been experiencing it along with you, like for the first time in years I've been enjoying everything for *me*," he explained. "This time of year was always hard for me because Alan and I had a New Years wedding. He used to call me his holiday husband. But this year... I've been happy."

The two met each other's eyes, and held their gazes for perhaps a moment too long. One leaned in closer - or did they both? Carson suddenly felt very hot, and as if he were holding his breath.

They moved a little closer.

A little closer.

A bit closer.

Closer.

They were so close that Carson could feel the other man's breath dancing on his skin, but there was nowhere else he would have rather been.

The sleigh suddenly lurched to a stop, sending the two men jolting forward.

"Your stop, Dave!" Marshall called from the front.

The two looked up to see that they were in front of the bakery. They had been so wrapped up in the moment that they hadn't realized they had been so close. Dave got out first and helped Carson down, and the two waved the older man off.

They stood awkwardly - as two people who had just very nearly kissed might - as the sleigh continued on down the street and disappeared around a corner.

Carson cleared his throat. "I should be getting back."

"Did you want a ride?"

"Nah, it's a nice night." Carson looked up to the dark sky above them. "I want to enjoy the stars while I still can. I'll see you tomorrow though? Around five for a run-through before the main event?"

Dave nodded. "Yeah, yeah, sounds good."

He watched Carson walk down main street in the direction of the hotel. He took one last look as he unlocked the door of his business, and could have sworn the journalist had a skip to his step.

8

"Can you believe it's already Christmas Eve?" Carson asked in disbelief as the two sat for breakfast once more, this time without their respective computers. The journalist felt like this was the first time they were able to just sit and relax.

"I know!" Kristen replied. "We've only been stuck in this tiny hellhole for three weeks, it feels like so much longer!"

Her colleague wasn't amused. "I meant that it's just flown by."

"I know what you meant," she grinned as she flipped her long, dark hair behind her. "You're right, it has gone quicker than I thought. Though it's probably gone much faster for you."

Carson crossed his arms and sat back in the dining chair. "What's that supposed to mean?"

"Oh, nothing really," she replied with a mock innocence. "Just that you've had a constant companion nearly this entire time, and no, I don't mean myself."

He rolled his eyes. "Please."

She began to count on her fingers. "Let's see, there was cookie decorating, skating, sledding, town snowball fight, and what was last night? Oh right! Sleigh rides."

"I..."

"Oh! And there was the lights thing too, can't forget that!"

"Dave has definitely been an asset to our assignment," he conceded with carefully chosen words. "I really didn't expect to meet anyone like him here and-- *Don't give me that look!*"

Kristen had a smug, pleased look on her face that she tried, and failed, to keep down. "Hey, I'm not the only one who thinks that you two would be good together," she said defensively. "A certain hotel manager thinks so too."

"Traitor!" Elsie called from the bar against the back wall.

"I didn't name names, but if the shoe fits!" Kristen called back. She shook her head and clicked her tongue. "No privacy, I swear. You just never know who's listening these days." The woman leaned forward on the table. "Hey, remember how much you complained on the ride up here?"

Carson chuckled sheepishly. "I guess I did complain a bit."

Neither heard the front door of the building open in the lobby behind them.

"*A bit?* It was never ending!" She replied before she changed her posture and lowered her voice to match her friend's. "*My name's Carson and I'm a big hotshot journalist and I'm way too good for a town like this.*"

"I don't sound like that," he laughed, but joined in. "*I'm way too talented for a stupid little hicktown like this.*"

"*I only like big cities where **proper** civilization lives!*"

"*Small towns are for unsuccessful people who have given up on their dreams and happiness! It's where promising careers come to die.*"

As the two laughed, the front door quietly closed.

Kristen grinned from ear to ear at the memory. "You were absolutely insufferable."

"Joke's on me in the end though, isn't it?" He couldn't help but grin too. "Who would have thought that I'd actually like it here?"

"You like *someone* here," she corrected. "Oh barmaid! Another coffee, if you please!"

"You know where it is!" Elsie called back. "Help yourself!"

"You seem to have a friend as well," Carson pointed out as she stood up to go fill her cup.

"Yeah, I like her!" Kristen said brightly. "She's sassy, the world needs it."

On a table near where the dining room met the lobby, a lone box labelled *Sweet Dave's Sweet Treats* sat unnoticed.

Carson made his way down the bustling street towards the bakery. There was an extra spring in his step and though the cold air nipped at his face, he didn't mind a bit. If he knew how to whistle, he probably would have been. It was a good day, and he was excited for what the evening would bring.

His eyes lit up when he noticed Dave standing outside the bakery doors.

"Hey! I missed you this morning!" Carson called as Dave locked the door of his business.

"I didn't," he replied shortly.

Carson blinked, caught off guard by the sudden hostility. "I'm sorry?"

"I saw you and your colleague," Dave said curtly, brushing

past Carson and walking to a white truck parked on the street. "More importantly, I *heard* you."

The journalist was thoroughly confused. "Wait, sorry, heard what?"

"I know it doesn't seem like much, but this *hicktown* is my home, and I'm proud of it. I'm *proud* to live here," Dave spat. "And the people who live here? They're my friends and family, and not one of them have given up on life, or whatever."

Now, it clicked. "Wait, wait, wait, this is just a huge misunderstanding."

"I don't think there's really anything to misunderstand."

"Dave please, you don't understand..." Carson tried desperately to explain.

"Why? Because I'm a dumb redneck and not some... some... bigshot like you?"

Carson shook his head. "I never said that, and as for the rest, it was a joke!"

"Sure it was," Dave's tone was flat; it was obvious that he didn't believe the other man. He unlocked his truck, climbed inside, and slammed the door behind him.

"Dave!"

The furious baker rolled down his window as he started the engine. "I have to go pick up Stella. Here's what's going to happen; we're going to smile in front of her, pretend that nothing has happened, do the broadcast, and then I never want to see you again."

He didn't give the other man a chance to answer. He rolled his window back up, turned up his radio, and drove off leaving Carson confused and dejected.

9

"What's the deal with this town, Elsie?" Kristen asked curiously, leaning against the front desk and zipping up her camera bag.

"What do you mean?" The older woman asked in response.

"Well there's what, 2,000 people here?"

"I think it was about 3,500 at the last census, but yes, it's small if that's what you're getting at."

"You've got a cute but surprisingly big hotel, Dave bakes more than I thought it was possible for one human being to be able to, not to mention all the other little shops along the main strip..." Kristen trailed off, trying to find the right words. "How do you all stay open? In business?"

Elsie laughed as she turned to fully face the camera woman. "It is obvious that you're from the city, my dear. But, it's not the first time I've been asked that. You might have noticed there's no big mega centers, like Walmart, around?"

Kristen hadn't actually noticed, and mentally went over the layout of the town in her head. "We all buy from the 'little' shops for our daily needs and whatnot. But in terms of me, there's a few ski hills not far from here, so most of my clients come from that around this time of year."

"That makes sense, you're probably more affordable than the resorts."

"I count on it," Elsie nodded. "In fact, I'm practically fully booked at the moment."

"Wait, really?" Kristen looked around at the empty lobby. "I feel like we're the only ones here."

"Just because you and Mr. Davis keep odd hours doesn't mean everyone else does," Elsie teased. "Most of my skiers are gone most of the day, and they trickle in during the evening. Some of them join in the festivities."

An angry Carson burst through the front doors.

"Ah, speak of the devil!" Kristen grinned. "We were just..."

"We need to get back," he cut his friend off. "Pack up your things and meet me back here as soon as you can. We'll be checking out," he added to Elsie.

Kristen was stunned. "I'm sorry? We're going live in a couple hours, remember? The big unveiling and..." She trailed off as the blond man thumped up the wooden stairs towards his room. Kristen hooked a thumb in Carson's direction and turned to Elsie. "Right, I'm going to go deal with that. I have a feeling that you should call Dave."

Elsie nodded. "Yes, I have a feeling that you're right."

Kristen stood at the heavy wooden door. Behind it, she could hear a furious rustling and thumping. "Heyyyyy, buddy, can I come in? We should talk about this."

There was no answer, so she knocked on the door. It hadn't been properly closed, and it cracked open with the force. She took advantage of this and pushed it to poke her head in. "Carson?"

He was pulling clothing from the closet and throwing it into the open suitcase on his bed. "I told you that we need to leave," he snapped at her without looking her way.

"Yeah, but here's the thing," she replied as she walked into the room while he plucked items from his closet, "I rather like being employed, and if we don't do that broadcast, I will no longer be employed. Paychecks, y'know? They're great. They pay the bills."

"You'll be fine, your work is solid," he pushed past her into the bathroom where he began scooping up his toiletries and tossing them into his leather travel case haphazardly. "They'll just reassign you."

"Appreciate the compliment, but consider this then; I like working with *you*," Carson stopped what he was doing and looked at her incredulously. "I'm serious. If you don't do this broadcast tonight, they *will* fire you." He shrugged, and walked back towards the waiting suitcase. "Look, I know I rib you a lot - it's how I show affection - but I actually think you're really talented and I'd rather not see you throw that away."

He scoffed. "I wish the network thought that."

"They *do* think that, you dingus!" She exclaimed. "Why else do you think you still have a job?" Carson didn't answer. "Anyone else - *anyone else* - would have been fired on the spot! If you screw *this* up, you'll be showing them that you're not the talent they thought you were, is that what you want? To waste your second chance?" She could tell by the look on his face that the fight finally was gone, so she took it as a sign to press on. "Now, all things considered, I think you enjoy your job too, so what's going on that would make you jeopardize it?"

Carson slumped down onto the bed and dropped his arms limply into his lap. "Dave thinks I hate the town."

"Okay... but you really don't," she replied. "We just talked about this."

"No, I don't," he insisted, "but Dave heard us goofing around at breakfast this morning."

It began to make sense to her. "Oh no."

"So not only does he think I hate this town - which, that alone he sees as a grave personal insult - he also thinks I'm a liar when I try to explain." He took a deep breath, and slapped his knees. "It doesn't matter what he thinks. Alright, let's do the broadcast tonight and leave this stupid town right after."

"We just established that it's *not* stupid."

"It's stupid because Dave's here and he's stupid!"

"Ah, professional writers. So eloquent." Kristen crossed her arms. "Listen, I just saved you from throwing out your job, and I'm not going to let you throw away your love life too."

"Love life?" The journalist scoffed at his friend. "I've known him what, three weeks?"

The woman shrugged. "Sometimes, three weeks is enough."

Carson couldn't believe what he was hearing. "Since *when*?" He shook his head. "And since when do *you* believe that? This isn't a movie; things aren't going to just magically work out."

She held up a finger. "One - I never said it would magically work out, and two - I believe that since I've been filming you two." She grabbed his arm and pulled him to his feet. "C'mon, I have something to show you."

Carson soon found himself seated at the desk in his colleague's room while she opened her laptop. He drummed his fingertips against the surface impatiently.

"You know, you could have just brought this back to *my* room," he told her. "Laptops are portable, pretty nice feature."

"Oh, shush," she scolded him as she clicked around on the screen that she had turned away from him. "I couldn't trust you to stay, this last hour has been kind of a rollercoaster. Now," she slid the computer in front of him, "shut up and watch."

As the video began to play, a soft melody played over the footage of the crowd of people.

Carson looked up at her. "Cheesy music? Really?"

Kristen smacked his shoulder. "Pay attention!"

He looked back to the screen, and was greeted with the image of himself and Dave from what he recognized as the light festival. As the baker grabbed his hands, the footage slowed down, and for the first time, Carson was able to see the look that they had exchanged. The two men on screen locked eyes, and shared a moment of tender wonder as the lights came to life around them, before the embarrassment that was so burned into his memory took over.

It was sort of magical, Carson had to admit.

Next, the scene changed, and it was when Dave had been helping him ice skate. Carson's face was caught in a laugh as he watched the ice below him, while Dave had a gentle smile as he guided the both of them. That too had been a fun night, the journalist had to admit. The way Kristen had framed it made it look as though they were the only ones on the ice, lost in each other's company. That was the way it had felt. It was sweet and innocent, but also deeply intimate.

Carson felt an ache deep in his chest as the footage changed to a montage - overlapping moments of the two of them caught looking at one another. There were even moments that he hadn't thought Kristen had been filming, or even been around for, such as a shot of them inside the bakery laughing that had clearly been filmed through the window.

His eyes burned as they filled with hot tears.

"We don't see stuff like this in the moment," Kristen explained, "but it's there."

The first tear escaped down Carson's cheek. "Yeah," he choked out. "How can I fix this?"

"Honestly? I'm not sure. What I am sure of is that you need to stop listening to your stupid brain and start listening to your heart because it is all over your face right now," she advised as she passed him a tissue box.

In something of a daze, Carson returned to his own hotel room and sat down on his bed. What could he do? How could he possibly show Dave what he - and the town - meant?

His eyes drifted to his desk, one of the few things he hadn't yet cleaned off. On top of a stack of notes lay his gingerbread self that he had decorated after the light festival; it looked a little rough after three weeks, but was still mostly intact.

That gave him an idea.

10

Carson bolted down the street as fast as his legs would carry him. He'd never been much of an athlete, but he gave it his all as if running for a gold metal, only what was at stake was worth more to him than any prize could ever be.

Funny, the street had never seemed so long any of the other times he had walked down it.

His heart pounded in his throat as he wheezed for breath from burning lungs, but he pressed himself on.

He finally reached the bakery, and nearly ran right past it. Carson stumbled rather ungracefully back towards the wood and glass door. He knocked on it frantically.

"Dave!" He called out between gasping for breath, "Dave, please! Let me in!"

"Dad, is this dress good for TV?" Stella asked as she twirled in front of the table the model was on. Her father was hunched over it, busily making last minute adjustments.

"It looks great, Star," he replied flatly, but didn't glance up as he dusted everything with a thin layer of powdered sugar.

The girl stamped her foot. "You didn't even look!"

"No whining, Stella, Santa hates whining," he scolded before he took a moment and sighed. "I'm sorry, Star, I just want everything to be perfect. This is a big moment for us! You and your dress look lovely."

"It will be perfect!" Stella assured her father, oblivious to the underlying pain on his tired face.

Both jumped at the sound of banging on the door. "Dave!" They heard a muffled voice call. "Dave please! Let me in!"

"It's Carson!" Stella shrieked excitedly, bolting over to the door.

"He can wait outsid..." The words hadn't finished leaving his lips when the bells above the door chimed loudly.

"You're early!" Stella told the journalist as she peered past him out the door. "Where's the camera lady?"

"Kristen," Carson reminded her, stepping inside and trying to catch his breath.

"Oh yeah, I forgot," she giggled. "But where is she? We can't be on TV without her!"

"She's just packing up all her equipment and then she'll be here," Carson assured the girl. "I came early to talk to your Dad."

"Good luck, he's grumpy," Stella warned, and Dave rolled his eyes.

"I know, and it's my fault," Carson told her. He looked towards the back of the bakery where he could see the baker working away. "Dave?" The baker didn't answer, or acknowledge his presence at all. "Dave, please hear me out. I know I upset you, and I'm sorry."

When he didn't answer once again, his daughter crossed her arms. "Dad, you always said it's rude not to answer people when they're talking to you."

This time, Dave sighed heavily and set the sifter down. "You're right, Stella. It is rude. Why don't you go upstairs for a few minutes and make sure your room is ready for TV?"

Stella scrunched her face. "My room's not going to be on TV."

"It might be," Carson cut in, "TV is unpredictable sometimes. It's better to be prepared."

"He's the expert," Dave shrugged. "But go on."

"Okay." Stella reluctantly obeyed, and headed for the stairs. The two men stood in an uncomfortable and tense silence while they waited for the footsteps to disappear upstairs. Finally, they heard the creak and clicking of her door being shut.

Only then did Dave nod. "Alright. Say your bit."

Carson wet his lips with his tongue, choosing his words carefully. "I'm really sorry for what you heard this morning, but it was totally out of context."

"So you said earlier, but do you really expect me to believe that?" Dave asked.

"Expect? No," Carson replied sincerely. "But I hope that you might, because it's the truth." Dave's expression didn't change. "It was a joke, between Kristen and I. We were making fun of *me* because I *did* think that - all of it - before I got here. I was angry about this assignment. Really, really angry," he admitted sheepishly. "But then I met you, and suddenly it was the best assignment I could have ever been given."

The baker took this in and contemplated it for what felt like an eternity to the other man. "What did you do to get this assignment? What was your mistake?"

"I..." Carson sighed. He still didn't want Dave to know, but he supposed it was time to be completely open. "I had secured a big interview with the Miller-Jones couple."

Dave shrugged. "Is that supposed to mean something?"

Carson couldn't help a laugh of disbelief; he couldn't imagine not knowing about the case when it had been such a huge presence in his own life, journalist or not. "They're a couple who *allegedly* killed their three kids, it was a huge case, media frenzy. This interview was going to be a big deal. The network advertised and hyped it up everywhere for over a month. I mean they *really* pushed this thing. It was going to be live, that's important. You're not familiar with the case at all?"

The dark haired man shook his head. "No, I can't say I am."

"These two absolutely killed their kids, they're not innocent and there's really no doubt of that. Unfortunately, they were acquitted on a technicality. Both of them, free. That was huge in the media world, and everyone wanted a piece of them. Networks, journalists, photographers... *Everyone* wanted an exclusive with them."

"That's grim," Dave frowned, "but you got the interview?"

"Yeah, I did! ... But then I blew it," Carson explained. "I asked questions that weren't on the approval list, and I pressed too hard, and... they walked out three minutes into the interview."

The other man winced. "Ouch."

"Yeah. Naturally, gossip shows and blogs got a hold of the story and ran with it - and *I* was the story. You can imagine what my reputation was after that."

"Wow," Dave said. "I see where you went wrong."

"Besides everywhere, what's that?"

Dave smirked. "Never agree to live interviews." Carson chuckled half-heartedly. "Why didn't you tell me before?"

"Because... I liked that you were the one person who *didn't* know," he admitted. "You didn't see me as a screw up or a joke." Carson exhaled deeply as he walked over to the table and stood near Dave. He looked over the model wistfully. "I care about what you think about me, and I know that you care about what I think of Everwinter Valley."

"Carson," the other man tried to interject.

"The truth is that I actually do love this quiet little town, and I love this bakery, I love Stella, and I love you," he declared as he rummaged around in his coat pocket. He pulled out his gingerbread self and held it in his hand a moment. "Maybe that's too soon, and I'm sorry if it is, but that's how I feel. If this is home for you," Carson leaned in and placed the cookie against the front of the miniature bakery, "then it's home for me too."

The baker didn't answer, and Carson shifted uncomfortably on his feet. He went to leave, but Dave grabbed his hand and pulled him back close. The baker's dark eyes were holding back tears.

Dave swallowed the lump in his throat. "I love you, too. I-- I'm sorry I jumped to conclusions like that. When I heard the two of you... I don't know. It just ignited something. Like maybe that's how I had always expected you to feel, and hearing that was a confirmation. Like it had all been an act."

"It's not how I feel," Carson whispered back. "This, *right here*, is how I feel."

"Daddy! Mistletoe!" The two heard an excited voice from the stairs. Stella was watching intently, grinning at them through the railing.

Both men tilted their heads up to view the ceiling above them. Sure enough, hung on one of the low wooden beams was the infamous kissing plant; bright red berries, green leaves, and tied together neatly at the base with a festive bow.

"So there is," Dave laughed at the surprise of being caught under his own decoration. He looked back to the shorter man before him. "Who are we to spit in the face of tradition?"

Carson grimaced playfully as he moved in closer. "Please don't spit in my face."

Dave leaned in closer.

Carson leaned in closer.

Closer.

His heart leapt as their lips met tenderly, soft and light at first, but deeper as their enthusiasm took over. The baker pulled him closer, wrapping his arms around the journalist's waist. Carson's hands met Dave's shoulders, and held him tightly. They nuzzled their noses together when they pulled back and laughed breathlessly like giddy teenagers.

"Merry Christmas, Carson," Dave said softly.

From the staircase, Stella cheered gleefully at the sight. A loud banging on the door startled them, but they looked over to see Kristen peering through the window and giving them an ecstatic thumbs up with one hand, her camera in the other.

Carson just laughed and buried his face into Dave's chest.

"And now, we go to Carson Davis who is joining us live from the Christmas Eve festivities in Everwinter Valley. Carson?"

Carson listened to the voice in his earpiece giving his introduction as Kristen gave him a thumbs up signal from behind the camera.

"Merry Christmas, Philip," he said into the microphone in his hand as he stood outside the bakery and in front of the large shop window. "I'm here outside the local bakery, *Sweet Dave's Sweet Treats*, where the owner - you guessed it - David Sweet, is about to unveil his yearly Christmas masterpiece. It's a large, gingerbread recreation of the main street here in Everwinter Valley, and from the sneak preview I got earlier, I think you'll find it's very *sweet*."

He stepped aside and nodded to the baker in the window. Dave took one side of the sheet covering the model, and Stella took the other from the opposite side. The father and daughter team whisked the sheet off with a graceful ease, and all the townsfolk gathered behind Kristen applauded and cheered at the sight.

While there was a lot to see, Carson smiled softly at one new detail in particular.

At the ginger bakery, a ginger Dave and a ginger Stella stood on either side of the gingerbread Carson.

11

Epilogue

Everwinter Valley is a town that, like me, you'd probably never heard of until now. It's a small town - under five thousand residents - but that doesn't mean that it's not worthy of being known.

When it comes to Christmas, this town goes all out; from the abundance of decorations to the plethora of lights, there's no forgetting which holiday season it is. Hay rides, ice skating, snow-shoeing... there's no shortage of activities, for people of every age! Young and old, everyone gets involved.

The vibrant community has plenty to offer as well. Shopping? There's multiple unique shops that sell everything from freshly baked goods to ice skates to gloves - if you're like me and forget to pack them. There's even a bustling hotel, which serves fine cuisine that would rival resorts ten times the price. Owner Elsie makes certain of that!

In the end, that's what truly makes Everwinter Valley special - the people who live here. They're friendly, welcoming, and spread genuine joy wherever you go.

Dave chuckled. "I think you're biased."

Carson shushed him.

If you ever want to experience true Christmas magic, Everwinter Valley has an authentic experience that isn't to be missed.

"Okay, now we can talk," Carson said.

"That's... it?"

"Yep, that was it."

"So... all that work... all this month... for a five minute segment?"

Carson nodded. "That's the job. It was only supposed to be a short assignment, remember, but then they wanted that stupid live broadcast."

"I don't think it was stupid," Dave said, grinning smugly and stretching back into the cushions of the couch. "In fact, I thought the subject matter was fascinating."

The smile was infectious and Carson couldn't help returning it. "It's true, I had a great star. Y'know," he mused, taking a sip of his hot chocolate, "I think Stella would be great in show business."

"Shh, not so loud, she'll hear you and it'll go right to her head," Dave hushed him teasingly. His smile faded just a bit. "When are you heading back to LA?"

Carson looked at him with a feigned bewilderment. "Did you not hear me yesterday? I live here now. Here here. Your home is mine. Already checked out of the hotel. I like eggs for breakfast."

The baker laughed. "That's doable, this is a bakery after all. I have no shortage of eggs."

"After New Years," Carson answered honestly, "though I was serious about maybe moving here. Depends on how good your eggs are, though. For now," he leaned back, and snuggled against the other man with his mug firmly in his hands, "I just want to enjoy being here."

At long last, both his mind, and his heart, were at rest.

About the Author

B. A. Loudon is a Canadian author out of Calgary, Alberta. Her first book released in June of 2019 while she was in hospital recovering from two emergency surgeries.

Her second book released in September 2019 and was far less dramatic.

She usually has 5-6 novels on the go at any given time, and frankly, it's a miracle that she finishes any of them. See next page for proof.

Find her online at

www.Baloudonwrites.com

12

Coming Soon

Everwinter Valley Series:

The Holiday Husband
The Winter Wedding Wife (TBA)

Music To Me Series:

The Metal Merch Girl (TBA)
Pop Punk Paradise (TBA)
My Five Boyband Boyfriends (TBA)
Country Music, City Girl (TBA)

Want a chance to read new novels before anyone else?
Don't forget to sign up for the mailing list!

13

From 'The Winter Wedding Wife'

"I don't like surprises, I like plans."

"Well, plan on being surprised then."

Carson didn't have time to plan anything. The spacious hotel dining room was illuminated by hundreds of candles spread throughout the room. Vibrant red rose petals lined the hotel's hardwood floors, while bouquets of various white flowers filled every table.

It was overwhelmingly beautiful.

But one thing was very certain; they certainly weren't there for a new menu tasting.

"Dave... what's going on?" Carson asked, looking around the room in awe and confusion.

Nine year old Stella emerged from the kitchen doors, and she was dressed in her best formal gown - a green and white lace dress that Carson had gotten her for a photoshoot in the bakery. Her hair was done in a neat updo, and she looked as elegant as everything else in the room.

"Dad and I have a question for you!"

The journalist had an inkling of what was coming. "Oh, do you now?"

"Yes, and it was important that we asked you together," Dave replied, taking his daughter's hand with his left hand and pulling a ring out from his pocket with his right. They both knelt down on one knee, well rehear "Carson Davis..."

"Will you join our family..."

"...and marry me?"

Carson looked at the pair a moment, amusement pulling at his lips. As hard as he tried, he couldn't contain himself and erupted into uncontrollable laughter.